How the Bear Lost His Tail

Written by Susan Price
Illustrated by Sara Ogilvie

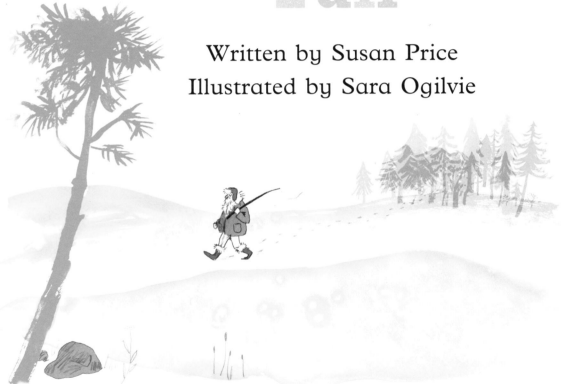

OXFORD
UNIVERSITY PRESS

We all know how bears are, don't we?

Bears are big, hairy and grumpy, with short, stumpy tails.
Bears weren't always like that though.
Once, long ago, bears were different.

2

They were still big and hairy, but they were sweet and kind, and had long, fluffy tails. Bears were proud of their tails in those days.

How did the bear get a stumpy tail?
Why are they so grumpy now?
Fox is to blame.

Let me tell you what Fox did.

Fox was trotting about one cold day, looking for something to eat.

He saw a fisherman by a frozen lake, dangling a line through a hole in the ice.

The fisherman had caught a lot of fish. They
were lying in the snow, tied together with string.
Fox was hungry.

Fox was sly and quick. He sneaked up, grabbed the string of fish, and ran as fast as he could!

In the forest, he met Bear. Bear was hungry too. He waved his long, fluffy tail and said, "Oh, Fox! Where did you get all those fish from?"

Fox saw that Bear's tail was even longer and fluffier than his.

Fox did not like that one bit. He did not want to share his fish either.

So Fox said, "I caught them!"

"How?" asked Bear.

"All you have to do is break a hole in the
ice on the lake," said Fox. "Then sit down and
put your tail in the water."

"It will be cold!" said Bear.
"Yes, but you will catch
a lot of fish! Sit still, and the
fish will come and nibble
your tail," said Fox.

"It might hurt, but don't pull your tail
out, or you will lose the fish! Your tail is so
long, you will catch even more than I did!"

"Oh, thank you, Fox!" said Bear.
"Remember, don't pull your tail
out too soon!" Fox said...

...and he ran on,
with his stolen fish.

Bear went down to the frozen lake. He did everything Fox had said. He broke a hole in the ice, and put his long, fluffy tail in the icy water.

It tingled. The water was cold! The tingling got worse as the fish began to bite. But Bear kept his tail in the water, just as Fox had said to do.

Ouch!

The water in the lake was so cold, the hole behind
Bear began to freeze over again.
But Bear did not see.

Bear had to grit his teeth. The more it tingled, the more fish he thought he was catching.

But soon it was too much for Bear.

"I don't care if I lose my fish. This hurts too much!" he thought.

He tried to pull his tail out of the water.

But his tail had frozen! It snapped off like an icicle, leaving nothing but a stump. He did not even have any fish.

Fox had made a fool of him.

From that day to this,
all bears have had short,
stumpy tails.

They are grumpy because
they think everyone is
laughing at them.

And Fox? Fox is still as quick and sly and clever as ever.

Bear, on the other hand, has learned that he shouldn't believe everything he is told.

Once upon a time...

The end.

💬 Tips for retelling the story

Talk about the story

- Ask your child to tell you why Fox decided to trick Bear. Ask: *What kind of character is Fox?*
- Look together at pages 16 to 20. Ask your child to suggest words that describe how Bear was feeling in the pictures on these pages, such as *freezing*, *hopeful*, *determined* or *annoyed*.
- Read the first sentence on page 6. Ask your child which word tells us how Fox was moving. Help them to identify *trotting*. Ask: *Can you think of any other words that could tell us how he moved?* E.g. *ran*, *crept*, *padded*.
- Ask: *Do you think this is really how bears came to have short stumpy tails?*

🔊 Retell the story using the story map

- Now you have read the story and talked about it, use the story map on page 24 to retell the story together. Each picture shows an important part of the story.
- Encourage your child to retell the story in their own words. You could do this together or take it in turns to tell different parts of it.
- As they retell the story, encourage your child to include descriptions of how both Fox and Bear were feeling as well as relating the events of the story.

OXFORD
UNIVERSITY PRESS

Great Clarendon Street, Oxford, OX2 6DP, United Kingdom

Oxford University Press is a department of the University of Oxford. It furthers the University's objective of excellence in research, scholarship, and education by publishing worldwide. Oxford is a registered trade mark of Oxford University Press in the UK and in certain other countries

Text © Susan Price 2011
Illustrations © Sara Ogilvie

The moral rights of the author have been asserted

First published 2011

British Library Cataloguing in Publication Data
Data available

ISBN: 978-0-19-833958-8

22

Typeset in Plantin Infant MT Std

Paper used in the production of this book is a natural, recyclable product made from wood grown in sustainable forests. The manufacturing process conforms to the environmental regulations of the country of origin.

Printed in Great Britain by Ashford Colour Press Ltd.

Oxford OWL

For school
Discover free eBooks, teaching notes, advice and support

For home
Helping your child's learning with free eBooks, essential tips and fun activities

www.oxfordowl.co.uk

Traditional Tales

How the Bear Lost His Tail

Fox is jealous of Bear's big, fluffy tail. So when Bear wants to catch some fish, sly Fox plays a trick on him.

Oxford Reading T

Oxford Level 6
Fully decodable

Book Band 6 Orange

Letters and Sounds Phas

Traditional Tales
Level 6

OXFORD
UNIVERSITY PRESS

How to get in touch:
web   www.oxfordprimary.co.uk
email schools.enquiries.uk@oup.com
tel.   +44 (0) 1536 452610
fax   +44 (0) 1865 313472

ISBN 978-0-19-833958

9 780198 339588

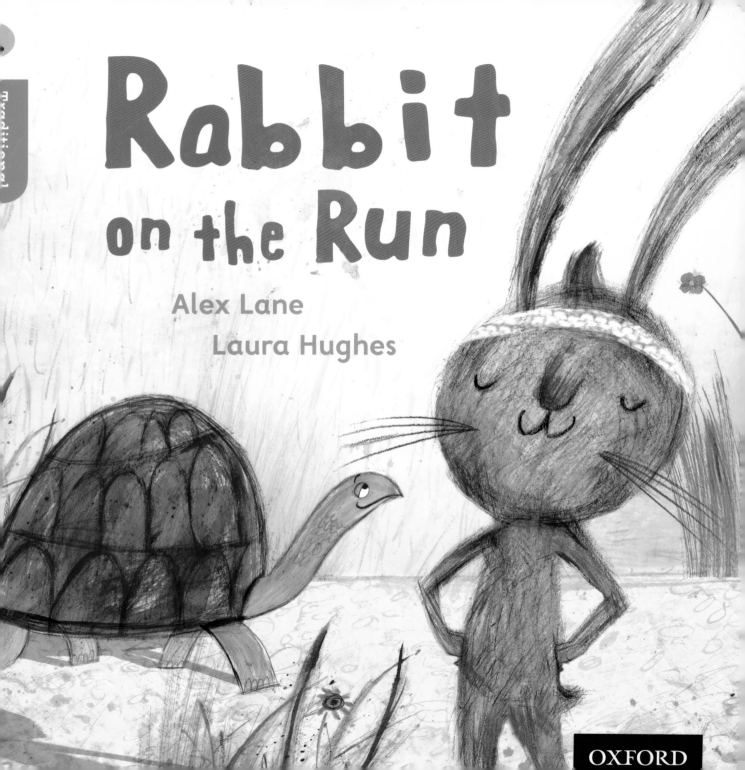

Rabbit
on the Run

Alex Lane

Laura Hughes

OXFORD

About the story

Traditional tales have been told for many years. This story is based on Aesop's fable The Tortoise and the Hare. Enjoy sharing and retelling this timeless story with your child again and again.

📖 Tips for reading together

Talk together

- Look at the cover of the book together and read the title. Ask: *Does Rabbit look like a good runner? Do you think he will win the race?*
- Look at pages 2 to 5 where the main characters are introduced and talk about the pictures. Ask: *What might the story be about?*
- Ask: *Do you like running races? Can you remember a time when you took part in a race?*

About the words in this story

- Your child will be able to read most of the words in this story using their phonics skills. Encourage your child to sound out and blend any new words.
- These words are common, but your child may find them tricky.

  me   was   you

  If necessary, read these words to your child.

During reading

- Encourage your child to read the story to you. Talk about the pictures with your child as they read.
- Encourage your child to say the sounds in a word, from left to right. Tell them to point to the sounds as they say them. Then they can blend the sounds into a whole word, e.g. *sh-o-t.*
- Give your child lots of time to sound out each word.
- Re-read the sentence encouraging your child to read with expression.
- Look out for repeated phrases, e.g. *You cannot get me!*

Use lots of praise to encourage your child!